THE THANKSGIVING MYSTERY

Joan Lowery Nixon

Pictures by Jim Cummins

ALBERT WHITMAN & COMPANY, CHICAGO

K
N

Library of Congress Cataloging in Publication Data

Nixon, Joan Lowery
  The Thanksgiving mystery

  (A First read-alone mystery)
  SUMMARY: With the help of a playful kitten,
Susan and Mike trick a "ghost" into revealing
himself.
  [1. Thanksgiving Day — Fiction. 2. Mystery
and detective stories] I. Cummins, James.
II. Title.
PZ7.N65Th   [E]   79-27346
ISBN 0-8075-7820-7

16555

To a special friend,
Colleen Scury

Did you see that?" Mrs. Pappas asked
Mike and Susan. "Something strange
went up the stairs and disappeared
at the top."

Mike and Susan stared upward. The light
at the top of the stairs was dim. They
couldn't see anything.

"What did the strange thing look like?"
Mike asked.

Mrs. Pappas shrugged. "It looked like someone wrapped in a white sheet."

Susan said, "That sounds like a ghost!"

"I hope there are no ghosts in our apartment house!" Mrs. Pappas said, quickly closing her door.

"Pete lives upstairs," Susan said. "Let's ask him if he's seen anything strange."

When Pete opened the door, Mike sniffed.
"I can tell your mother's baking pumpkin
pies for Thanksgiving! Do you think she'd
give out samples?"

"You're always thinking about food,"
Susan said to Mike. She turned
to Pete. "We came to ask if you've
seen a ghost up here."

"Susan thinks there's some dumb ghost
running around the apartment house,"
Mike said.

"There are no such things as ghosts!"
Pete grumbled. "And I'm too busy to talk
right now." He closed the door.

Susan and Mike looked at each other.
"I wonder what's wrong with Pete,"
Mike said.

"Maybe he's afraid of ghosts," said
Susan. "Let's ask Mrs. Pickett if she's
seen anything."

Mike and Susan went to Mrs. Pickett's apartment. Mrs. Pickett smiled when she opened the door. "Happy almost Thanksgiving!" she said. "You must come tomorrow to share some of the good things I'm making."

"I hope you're baking pumpkin pies," Mike said. He reached down to pet Mrs. Pickett's kitten, H.B. Mrs. Pickett had gotten the kitten on her birthday. "H.B." stood for "Happy Birthday."

"No," Mrs. Pickett said. "I don't like pumpkin pie. On Thanksgiving Day I make food I'm really thankful for, like caramel apples and bacon sandwiches."

"Mrs. Pickett, we came to ask you something important," Susan said.

"Another white whale riddle?" Mrs. Pickett asked. "Well, I've got one for you. Which side does a big white whale get the wettest?"

"I don't know. Which side?" Mike asked.

Mrs. Pickett giggled. "The outside!"

"This is serious, Mrs. Pickett. We want to ask if you've seen a ghost in the apartment house," Susan said.

"Is that what it was?" Mrs. Pickett
asked. "Yesterday evening, about seven
o'clock, I saw something white
dash out the front door."

Susan looked at Mike. "Thank you, Mrs.
Pickett." She pulled her brother into
the hall.

"Pete is right," Mike said. "There are no such things as ghosts."

"Maybe not, but there's something strange in the apartment house," Susan answered. "Mrs. Foshee lives upstairs. Maybe she's seen something, too. Come on, Mike!"

Mrs. Foshee invited Susan and Mike inside. She nodded as they told her about the ghost. "For two days I've heard strange grumbling, groaning noises in the hallway," she said. "Once I opened the door in time to see something white disappear down the stairs."

"Did you hear the noises about seven
o'clock?" Susan asked.

"Yes. And today I heard the same
thing again about two o'clock. But it
had gone by the time I opened my door."

16555

15

"What would a ghost want in our
apartment house?" Susan asked.

Mike laughed. "Maybe it's the ghost of
a Pilgrim, back for another Thanksgiving
dinner."

"I don't think a Pilgrim ghost would be
hungry," Mrs. Foshee said. "That first
Thanksgiving dinner lasted three days.
The Pilgrims and their Indian guests
ate so much there wasn't enough food
left to last the winter."

"It's a good thing Mike wasn't with them," Susan said. "There wouldn't have been *any* food left."

"If you see the ghost, why don't you ask him why he's here?" Mrs. Foshee said.

"We will," Susan said.

"I don't think I want to see a ghost," Mike muttered.

When Susan and Mike were back in the
hall, Susan said, "For two days the ghost
has gone down the stairs at seven
o'clock."

"Today Mrs. Foshee saw him going
downstairs at two o'clock, and Mrs.
Pappas saw him going up the stairs at
about four o'clock," Mike said.

"If Mrs. Pappas saw him going upstairs, then he must be somewhere in the apartment house now," Susan said.

She and Mike looked around nervously.

"Do you think the ghost will go out again at seven o'clock?" Mike whispered.

Susan nodded. "We need to think of some place to hide."

"How about under a bed?" Mike suggested.

"No," Susan said. "We need to find a hiding place where we can see the ghost."

"We could see the stairway from the broom
closet near Mrs. Pickett's," Mike said.
"Maybe she'd come with us. I bet she's
not afraid of ghosts."

Susan and Mike ran down the stairs to
Mrs. Pickett's apartment.

"I've got another white whale riddle," Mrs.
Pickett said as she opened her door.
"Do you know why a big white whale never
goes swimming on an empty stomach?
Because it's easier to swim in water!"
She laughed so hard she had to wipe
her eyes.

"That's a good riddle," Susan said.
"But listen to our plan." Then she
and Mike told Mrs. Pickett about
their idea to watch for the ghost.

"I'll be glad to help you in your
detective work," Mrs. Pickett said.
"I can't wait to catch the ghost!"

21

At fifteen minutes to seven, Susan, Mike, Mrs. Pickett, and H.B. hid inside the broom closet. They peeked through a crack in the door.

All of a sudden, Susan whispered, "Listen! I think I hear the ghost!"

From somewhere above the stairway came a groan, then a low, muttering, grumbling sound.

As Susan and Mike watched, a white shape
appeared in the dim light at the top of
the stairs. The shape began to come down
the steps toward them. It moved slowly,
making a loud thumping noise.

Mike felt something soft brush against his legs. He looked down, then grabbed Susan's arm. "Oh, no! There goes H.B." The kitten darted out the door. He ran to the bottom step and sat down.

"What if the ghost steps on H.B.?" Susan asked. She knew she should do something, but she was too frightened to move.

Thump, thump, thump, the ghost kept coming. H.B. sat still, right in its way.

Susan put her face in her hands. "I can't look," she whispered.

All of a sudden, H.B. screeched, "Yeow!" He jumped straight up in the air. The ghost sat down on the stairs with a thud. A white sheet slid to the floor.

"That's not a ghost! It's a giant turkey!" Susan shouted. A large brown bird sat on the steps, flapping its wings. A few feathers fluttered in the air.

Mrs. Pickett, Mike, and Susan hurried into the hall.

"It's not a turkey," Mike said. "It's
Pete!" Mike began to laugh. "Pete,
what are you doing in that crazy
turkey costume?"

Pete pushed a feather out of his face.
He glared at Mike. "My mother is making
me be in a Thanksgiving play for her
club. I didn't want anyone to see me
in this dumb costume when I went to
rehearsals. I didn't want people to laugh."

"Were your rehearsals every night at
seven?" Mike asked.

"Yes," Pete said. "And we had to go
this afternoon, too." He groaned
again. "This costume is so tight it
gives me a stomachache."

"So that's why everyone heard groans," Mike said.

"I guess so," Pete said.

"I'm just glad to find a turkey instead of a ghost," said Susan. "And I'd like to see the play."

Pete looked happier. "It's in half
an hour. Do you really want to come?"

"We all want to see your play, Pete,"
Mrs. Pickett said. "And afterwards we'll
come back to my apartment for some
caramel apples."

She smiled. "What an exciting
Thanksgiving party I'll have, with two
detectives and a ghost!"

F
N

Nixon, Joan Lowery.

**The Thanksgiving
mystery.**